Dad Mops

Written by Roisin Leahy

Illustrated by Celia Ivey

Collins

tin cans

ticks

tin cans

ticks

a pan

the dog kicks

a pan

the dog kicks

a sack

dad mops

· · · · · · ·

a sack

dad mops

14

ck

15

 Review: After reading

Use your assessment from hearing the children read to choose any GPCs, words or tricky words that need additional practice.

Read 1: Decoding

- Use grapheme cards to make any words you need to practise. Model reading those words, using teacher-led blending.
- Look at the "I spy sounds" pages (14–15) together. Ask the children to point out as many things as they can in the picture that begin with the /c/ sound. (*cap, cat, clap, cake, camera, carrots, cucumber, corn, cards, cups, crayons*) Repeat for things that end in "ck". (*socks, click (camera), clock, backpack/rucksack, truck*)
- Ask the children to follow as you read the whole book, demonstrating fluency and prosody.

Read 2: Vocabulary

- Look back through the book and discuss the pictures. Encourage the children to talk about details that stand out for them. Use a dialogic talk model to expand on their ideas and recast them in full sentences as naturally as possible.
- Work together to expand vocabulary by naming objects in the pictures that children do not know.
- On pages 2 and 3, ask the children to explain what is in the **tin cans**. (e.g. *fruit, things to make the cake*) Ask: What else have you seen in tin cans? (e.g. *soup, beans, corn*)

Read 3: Comprehension

- Talk about baking cakes or similar. Ask: Have you helped get food for special occasions? What sort of things would you like to bake or cook? What special occasion could you cook for?
- Reread pages 2 and 3. Ask: Do you think the girl has the things on the list? Why? (e.g. *yes, she has ticked them*) What does she need these things for? (e.g. *to make a birthday cake*)
- Reread pages 10 and 11. Ask: What did Dad do? (e.g. *mop up the mess*) What made the mess? (e.g. *the dog*)